Oh, Brother!

Adapted by Katherine Emmons and Claire Roman
Illustrated by Todd Bright
Art crafted by Winnie Ho
Inspired by the art and character designs created by Pixar

A Random House PICTUREBACK® Book

Random House 🏠 New York

Library of Congress Control Number: 2007920067
ISBN: 978-0-7364-2432-5

www.randomhouse.com/kids/disney

Printed in the United States of America
10 9 8 7 6 5 4 3 2 1

Hi. My name's Emile. I'm the big rat. See that serious little guy over there to the right? That's Remy. He's my big brother. I know, I know. You're gonna say I'm **BIG** and he's little. But he's older than I am, okay? Anyway, this is our story—well, at least part of it.

Once upon a time, my brother Remy and I lived in the country in this old woman's attic. That was when we discovered that Remy had a taste for fine food and an amazing sense of smell. He could even sniff out good food from bad and tell whether it was safe to eat. Pretty impressive for a little rat, huh?

Remy was always on the lookout for good food. And that was always **getting me into trouble.** Take, for example, the time he decided to make a mushroom-cheese melt on the roof. Sounds fun, right? Wrong! Suddenly—ZAP!—we got hit by lightning.

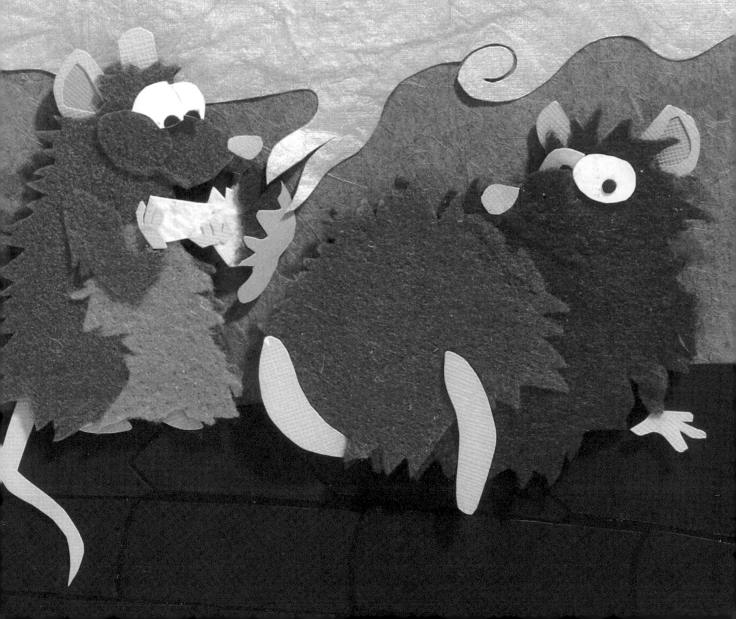

Remy didn't love just food. He loved cooking, too. And he didn't care if it put him—or me—in danger! So he dragged me into the old woman's kitchen to grab a spice *while she was napping*! Then he showed me this cookbook! Huh? Remy could read a book? Humans read, not rats!

And as if that wasn't enough, when Remy heard the voice of his favorite chef on TV, he raced over to watch. That was a big mistake. The old woman woke up—and let's just say we all had to leave in a hurry that day!

We ran away into the sewers—and that was when I lost Remy. It was pretty sad. But one night, we accidentally crossed paths. It was great to see the little guy again. I was so happy that I led him home—you know, to the sewers.

Of course, he had to do that weird thing—walking like a human, on two legs instead of four. All I could think was **"He'd better not let Dad see him do that!"**

I thought Remy would love the sewers. And he did. But there was this problem: he had gotten used to living with humans. He would still visit us, but he had to go back to them.

You see, Remy actually **liked** living with humans.

If you ask me, humans are scary. I don't know about you, but when I see humans, I hide. Remy isn't afraid of them at all.

And that wasn't the worst of it. Remy had begun this ritual of **washing** himself regularly! Can you believe it? A **clean** rat!

Me? I'm different (as you can see).
"What's wrong with a little dirt?" I
always say.

One day, Remy needed our help in his human world, so we all pitched in to cook. I wasn't so sure about that. But Remy's my brother, so what could I do? I can't say **NO** to him!

Now he cooks, and I eat. Yeah, Remy and I are a little different, but—aw, heck, what can I say? He's the best little older brother a rat could have.

Hey! There's the little guy right now. It looks as if he heard that part about his being the best brother a rat could have—uh-oh. Is that a hug see coming my way? *Oof!*

OH, BROTHER!